It Was You, Blue Kangaroo!

Emma Chichester Clark

Andersen Press
LONDON

for Jack Brown,
Lily's
little brother

First published in Great Britain in 2001 by Andersen Press Ltd., 20 Vauxhall Bridge Road, London SW1V 2SA.
Published in Australia by Random House Australia Pty., 20 Alfred Street, Milsons Point, Sydney, NSW 2061.
 Colour separated in Switzerland by Photolitho AG, Zürich. Printed and bound in Italy
by Grafiche AZ, Verona.

10 9 8 7 6 5 4 3 2

British Library Cataloguing in Publication Data available.

ISBN 1 84270 023 5

This book has been printed on acid-free paper

Blue Kangaroo belonged to Lily.
He was her very own kangaroo.
Sometimes, when Lily was very naughty she would say,
"It was you, Blue Kangaroo!"
And Blue Kangaroo would look at Lily, but say nothing.

One day, Lily decided to give all her dolls a bubble bath.

She filled the kitchen sink with soapy water and gave them a good scrub.

Then she went to get a towel . . .

. . . and Blue Kangaroo
wondered if the water
would stop coming.

“Lily!” cried her mother. “Who left the tap running?”
“It was you, Blue Kangaroo!” said Lily.
Blue Kangaroo looked at Lily, but he said nothing.

The next day, Lily found some old baby clothes which would be just the right size for the cat.

But when it came to the knickers,
he wriggled . . .

. . . and Blue Kangaroo
didn't like all the
snarling noises.

Suddenly the cat went mad. He flew out of Lily's arms . . .

. . . and landed on the curtains. Everything came crashing down.

“Lily!” cried Lily’s mother.
“It was you, Blue Kangaroo!” said Lily.
Blue Kangaroo looked at Lily, but he said nothing.

Lily took Blue Kangaroo out into the garden.
Her little brother was playing in the sandpit.
He was perfectly happy.

“I want to play with that!” said Lily.
“No! Mine!” wailed her little brother.

He screamed and screamed . . .

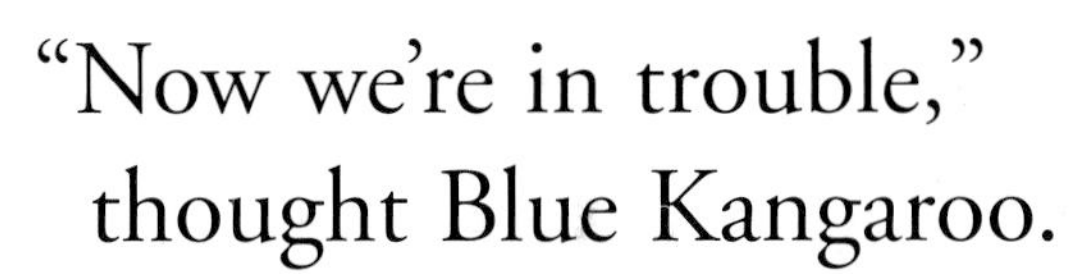

"Now we're in trouble,"
thought Blue Kangaroo.

"Lily!" said Lily's mother. "Who did this?"
"It was you, Blue Kangaroo!" said Lily.

"Well, you'd better take him to your room and stay there until I say he can come down," said Lily's mother.
Blue Kangaroo looked at Lily, but he said nothing.

Lily stayed upstairs with Blue Kangaroo.
She decided to take everything out of
the drawers . . .

. . . and throw it all away.

Blue Kangaroo
didn't dare look.

“Ooooh!” cried Aunt Jemima.
“LILY!” shouted Lily’s mother.

"Which of you threw these?" asked Lily's mother.
"It was you, Blue Kangaroo!" said Lily.
Blue Kangaroo looked at Lily, but he said nothing.

"Well, if Blue Kangaroo can't behave he'll have to sit by himself downstairs," said Lily's mother. And she put him on top of the bookcase, out of reach.

That night, Lily refused to go to bed.
"I never sleep without Blue Kangaroo!" she said.
But Lily's mother was firm.

"I'm sorry, Blue Kangaroo . . ." sobbed Lily.
And she cried herself to sleep.

Poor Blue Kangaroo!
He sat alone in the dark,
wide awake and thinking.

Then, he had an idea . . .

He found a pencil and a piece of paper,
and he began to draw.

When he had finished, he crept upstairs and slid
the piece of paper under Lily's mother's door.

Then he hopped back on top of the bookcase,
and waited.

"What a lovely surprise, Lily," said her mother.
"Who drew this?"

Lily looked at the picture.
"It was you, Blue Kangaroo!"
she whispered.
And Blue Kangaroo smiled,
but he said nothing.